Ozora Stearns Davis, William Drummond Baker

Dartmouth Lyrics

Ozora Stearns Davis, William Drummond Baker

Dartmouth Lyrics

ISBN/EAN: 9783744769167

Printed in Europe, USA, Canada, Australia, Japan

Cover: Foto ©Andreas Hilbeck / pixelio.de

More available books at **www.hansebooks.com**

DARTMOUTH LYRICS

A COLLECTION OF POEMS FROM THE UNDERGRADUATE PUBLICATIONS OF DARTMOUTH COLLEGE

EDITED BY

OZORA STEARNS DAVIS, '89

AND

WILLIAM DRUMMOND BAKER, '89

CAMBRIDGE
Printed at the Riverside Press
1888

CONTENTS.

iv CONTENTS.

CONTENTS.

INTRODUCTION.

DARTMOUTH journalism made a feeble beginning in 1835 with the *Magnet*. The publication of this sheet, with that of the *Scrap-Book*, two years later, was continued only for a few numbers. In 1839 the *Dartmouth* first appeared, at that time in the form of a monthly magazine of an exclusively literary character. The graduation of the class of 1843 saw the cessation of this first series. From this time until 1867 there was no established college paper, though several were begun. In January of that year, the second series of the *Dartmouth* began, and was continued in the monthly form until December, 1874. The *Anvil*, a weekly paper published during the single college year of 1873–4, was a decided success, and opened up for the college a new field — that of the college newspaper. As a result, in 1874 the *Dartmouth* began its third series as a weekly, containing little but news. Finally, in 1879 it was again changed to its present form, a bi-monthly, containing both news and literary matter. In 1886 appeared the *Dartmouth Literary Monthly*, edited by a board from the senior and junior classes. Its aim, like its name, is that of a purely literary magazine.

Our college verse, even more than its prose, has felt the influence of the times. In the course of an examination, one detects the influences of Tennyson, Wordsworth, Bryant, Longfellow, and latterly of Swinburne and the host of writers of *vers de société*, represented by Austin Dobson. The older poetry was ambitious in its aim, and as a consequence fell farther short of its mark than later more modest and natural work. Few poems in this collection were written more than a dozen years ago. Again, as a result of the artistic and highly finished work done everywhere of late years, college verse has become more carefully written and exact in form. By far the best of our undergraduate poetry is the product of the last four years.

Every one knows the limitations and failures of college verse, even at its best. But we hope that those into whose hands this volume may fall will find it, while not a perfect collection, yet what the editors have earnestly tried to make it, a faithful representative of Dartmouth's best work in poetry.

While a few of the earlier poems here collected cannot, in perfect strictness, be called lyrics, yet the editors have felt that the exceptions were so few that in giving the volume a title they might be overlooked.

We desire to take this opportunity to thank Professor M. D. Bisbee, the librarian of the college, for the free use of the files of the college journals, and Professor C. F. Richardson, for valuable aid in the preparation of this volume.

O. S. DAVIS,
W. D. BAKER.

HANOVER, N. H., *November, 1888.*

When morning floods the waiting hills **with**
    light

And, step by step, **drives down the** rebel
    gloom,

The woods reëcho, with a trebled might,

The music, ringing through their leafy room.

When flowers feel **no** blight nor lack of
    bloom,

When hope has **known no** loss nor death **to**
    mar,

In joy and strength we hail the dawn afar,

And, through the growing hours **of** life's
    sweet day,

We sing our songs **of** love **and mirth** —
    though far

From perfect be our morning's happy **lay.**

DARTMOUTH LYRICS.

I.

ERATO.

OVELY Muse of god-born race !
Oft I see thy Grecian face,
Oft I gaze in those fond eyes
Soft and blue as Lemnian skies.

But those lips for me are still,
Speak to me they never will :
Lips I never saw like thine,
Red as reddest Lesbian wine.

In thy rose-wreathed, wavy hair
Eros weaves for me a snare,
And the music of thy lyre
Fills my throbbing heart with fire.

Ah ! could I thy praise prolong
In an endless strain of song,

Could my tongue the numbers tell
Which my burdened spirit swell,

Then would I forevermore,
On the old Ægean shore,
By the sounding, purple sea,
Linger still and sing for thee.

II.

SQUAB FLIGHTS.

"LOVE is eternal," sang I long ago
    Of some light love that lasted for
        a day;
    But when the fleeting fancy passed
        away,
And other loves, that following made as
    though
They were the very deathless, lost the glow
    Youth mimics the divine with, and grew
        gray,
    I said, "It is a dream: no love will stay."
Angels have taught me wisdom. Now I
    know,
Though lesser loves and greater loves may
    cease,
    Love still endures, knocking at myriad
        gates
    That lead to God — stars, winds and waters,
        birds,

Beasts, flowers and men — speaking its sweetest words
  At woman's portal, till it finds its peace
  In the abyss where Godhead loves and
   waits.

                             Richard Hovey.

III.

EVEN-SONG.

WITH noiseless tread
    The dewy dusk has gently swung
    The flaming red
And purple gates; and high among
The stars the harvest moon is hung.

Dim clouds of white
Are chasing shadows past the dell.
    With whispers light
The little trees above me tell
A story that I know so well;

    For oh, behold!
The clouds have left a radiant ring —
    A crown of gold;
And there in beauty night doth bring
My love.   For joy my heart doth sing!
                William Drummond Baker.

IV.

AT THE TRYSTING-PLACE.

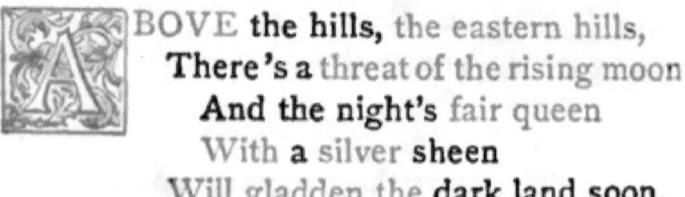

BOVE the hills, the eastern hills,
   There's a threat of the rising moon;
      And the night's fair queen
      With a silver sheen
   Will gladden the dark land soon.

Above the hills the white light fills
   The vast, star-studded dome,
      Then, into sight,
      A disc of light,
   She swings from her eastern home.

And through the trees, the evening breeze
   Sings a welcome to greet the light;
      Furious and long
      Is the rasping song
   Of the cricket minstrels of night.

Rise higher, O Moon, above the hills !
   Sigh softly, O evening Breeze !
My throbbing heart with longing thrills
   As I wait beneath the trees.

Crickets, chirp low !
Her haste **is** slow !
Now, over the meadow, I **see**
A queen in white :
In the growing night
My love has come to **me**.

Ozora Stearns Davis.

V.

THE GUIDE-BOARD SPEAKS.

The guide-board is hanging in the room of a sophomore, surrounded by signs, handkerchiefs, and other souvenirs of his conquests.

N honored place of old was mine,
　　Beside the highway stañding;
　　Four miles, I said, to Thompson's
　　　　Mills,
And six to Bowker's Landing.

The weary traveller, on the road,
　　To me his thoughts addressing,
Found out the way to Thompson's Mills,
　　And gave his heartfelt blessing.

I loved to see the children pass,
　　And hear their artless prattle,
The lumbering stage-coach and its load,
　　With many a jounce and rattle.

The deacon on his way to church,
　　Looked up with friendly greeting.

Two lovers at my mossy foot
    Once had their place of meeting.

But now I hang in durance vile,
    The butt of jests and slander,
That I who showed the way so long,
    Should to such nonsense pander !

I long to hear the song of birds,
    And catch the breath of clover.
Alas ! my hopes are all in vain,
    My usefulness is over.

EPITAPH.

An honored place of old was mine,
    Beside the highway standing;
Four miles, I said, to Thompson's Mills,
    And six to Bowker's Landing.
                        Newton Marshall Hall.

VI.

WAITING.

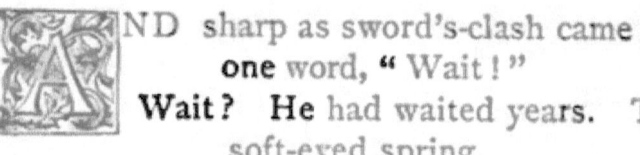

ND sharp as sword's-clash came the
     one word, " Wait ! "
     Wait ?   He had waited years.   The
          soft-eyed spring,
Crowned with sweet daisies and forget-me-
          nots,
The June with roses slumbering in her hair,
The blithe October with his grape-stained face,
And winter with a winding-sheet of snow,
Had passed him by with tiresome, steady pace,
Year after year, and found him waiting still.

O God, 't is hard to wait ! to stand one side
And see the noisy crowd go battling on ;
To mark that other hands, less strong than his,
Grasp the bright crowns that gleam for him in
          vain ;
To note the love-light shining in some face, —
A face Madonna-like in its repose, —
And know that not for him was human love ;
To yearn, and long, and pray for — yet to *wait.*

Once he had toiled for gold; had watched the
    pile
Of glittering coin grow 'neath his stealthy
    touch,
Had envied e'en the happy summer fields,
The buttercups that sparkled here and there;
Had measured with the yard the rainbow arch,
And coined his life out till it seemed spun
    gold.
And then came loss by flood and field and fire;
The storm-winds beat upon his earthly home,
The red flames crackled 'round his shining
    store,
With impish laughter clapping their red
    hands;
And in and through and over all His voice
Saying, "Be still and know that I am God!
This is the end — stand back and humbly
    wait!"

Then he had lived for fame, had sold himself
To what he called "the people." And the
    world —
The busy, heartless world that stands one
    side,
And claps or frowns as suits its whim the
    best —
Cheered on, cried "Good!" and "Brave phi-
    lanthropist!"
"This man has packed the truth into a shell,

Which — look you — now he offer us to crack;
We'll give him honors and a seat of state."
Ah ! he had labored nights, and watched the
     hours
Creep heavy-footed down the halls of time;
Had heard the deep bells on the frosty air
Ring out the hours, and then had gone to rest
With aching head and eyes too dull for
     sight; —
And all for what ? To see the great wave
     turn
And beat him back upon the barren shore;
To hear men praise another — yes, and jeer,
And call him fool, whom yesterday the fates
Had seemed to beckon on with waving hands,
And jewelled hair, and gleams of flashing eyes;
And then that word, as if an angel spoke, —
Solemn, yet not without its comfort, too, —
The peace of that word fell upon him —
     "Wait !"

The June was with him. All the summer air
Was full of fragrance blown from the sweet-
     brier,
And rich with melody that ne'er was wrought
By cunningest musicians ; humming bees
Rocked in the golden heart of flowers all day;
And when the night climbed up the sunset
     hills,

Leaving behind her train of silver stars,
The ghostly moon shone down through linden-
    trees,
And God's great peace found rest within his
    soul.

And June and roses and the birds brought
    love.
Oh, she was fair as lily on its stalk
Or sweet white clover which the zephyr bends,
With face that soothed you like a low, sweet
    psalm,
To mark her saint or else some pure Madonna.
The June had faded, and the autumn winds
Rustled the dead leaves round a new-made
    grave,
O'er which a marble angel drooped her wings.
The old, old story, old as death and time,
The one is taken and the other left,
While to his heart descends the solemn words,
"Thy time shall come, not now, but quickly
    — Wait !"

The slow years dragged along, month after
    month,
Week following week ; and each slow-footed
    day
Found him the same, yet changed.   The coun-
    try folk
Told tales of how much good he did the poor,

How kind he was, how gently soft he spoke,
Most often, too, to children, and to those
Whom grief had touched ; and oftentimes,
        they said,
His face was as an angel's, with the light
(That never shone on land nor yet on sea)
About the eyes; a certain longing, too,
As if he hoped for something that should be
If not on earth, yet in eternity.

They say his death was like a little child's.
The snow was hovering in the wintry air,
The winds were chanting in the leafless trees
A solemn music ; and as the red sun
Sank 'neath the hills, he turned away his face,
The sweet smile haunting still the kindly
        lips
And tender eyes, and cried, "At last ! at last
The watch is over !" and then fell asleep.

                          John Adams Bellows.

VII.

THE WITCHES.

SCENE, *a professor's study. Night. Cauldron in the middle. Thunder. Enter three witches.*

1*st W.* Thrice a freshman loud has cursed !

2*d W.* Once hath shrieked the sophomore's horn !

3*d W.* 'T is midnight's hour ! to work, to work !

1*st W.*   Dance around the cauldron dread.
    Curses on the wretch's head,
    Who incurs our baleful spell;
    Tongue can ne'er its horrors tell !
    In the grim digamma throw !
    Therein too καὶ γάρ must go !

All. Crush the heart and rend the brain,
    Victims quickly drive insane !

2*d W.* Marks of deadly Persian hate,
    Clisthenes' reforms of state,
    Force of ἄν and suffix θεν,
    Relics of the Hydra's den,

Golden fleece, the Argo's course,
And the probable Greek force,
Use of μέν and use of δέ,
Derivation, too, of γε,
Meaning of enclitic κε,
Pericles' and Solon's fame,
Origin of Plato's name,
Dative case of pronoun σύ,
Credit to Tyrtæus due :
With this mass of horrors grim,
Fill the cauldron to the brim !

All.   Crush the heart and rend the brain,
Victims quickly drive insane !

2d W. Stir the dreadful compound long,
Make our charm thus doubly strong !

Enter Professor.

Prof.   Well done ! your deeds my soul de-
light !
With your decoction to the fight !
Accursed papers fraught with fear,
Steeped in the mixture I revere,
Would wring from stony eyes the tear !

VIII.

THE BATTLE OF TOURS.

 HEARD the roar of battle down
   the past,
And vaguely saw, through mists of
  flying years,
Huge forms, strange banners borne along the
  blast
'Mid gleaming ranks of spears, ·

Squadrons in shining mail, with turbans
  crowned,
Long streams of yellow hair, and blazing eyes,
And crimson pools upon the trembling
  ground,
And arrow clouded skies,

And white arms tossed upon the wailing wind,
And breasts, where sons of heroes should
  have lain,
Go down beneath the horse's hoof — to find
Rest on a heap of slain.

And through the dim, wide portals of the night,
Silent and slow the crescent sank, blood-
    stained;
And when the northern trumpet hailed the
    light
The cross alone remained :

Its broad'ning shadows stretched across the
    land,
Westward beyond the arch of unknown seas ;
In its blest shade rise states and cities grand,
Float priceless argosies,

Round rusty cannon children laugh and sing,
The golden horn of plenty fills and swells,
And lovers' happy voices sweetly ring
Like distant sounding bells.

IX.

ON THE RIVER.

DRIFTING downward with the river
　　Past the willows on the shore,
　　Watching　for　the　moon - beam's
　　　　quiver
In the ripple round the oar,

Dreaming, in the peaceful quiet
　　Of the summer evening's air,
Tender fancies, running riot,
　　Far from life and light and care;

Thus we floated on together,
　　Joyous as the stars above;
Talking little of the weather,
　　Whispering low our words of love.

Lip to lip the compact sealing,
　　Homeward now; the voyage is done.
But the merry chimes are pealing
　　"She is won!" Yes, she is won.

X.

DRIFTING.

SEA, thy waves are merciless and
      wild ;
Across thy trackless waste no sun-
      shine gleams,
Nor peaceful moon, with white effulgence
      mild,
Filling the night with glory, till it seems
Only the dawn of a diviner day.
Thy solitude is one eternal night,
Whose blackness is unlit by heaven's ray,
And on thy billows we, bereft of sight,
The helpless driftwood of the changing years,
Rush on, now side by side upon the crest,
Now dashed apart amid the spray of tears,
Never to meet or from our drifting rest,
Till all that floats upon the mighty sea
Reaches the haven of eternity !

XI.

ON THE COAST.

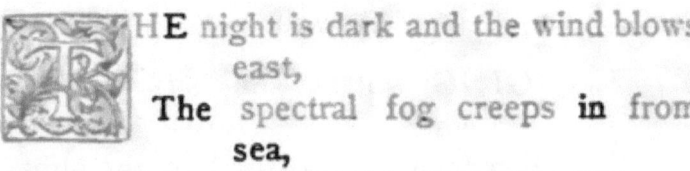

THE night is dark and the wind blows
    east,
  The spectral fog creeps in from
    sea,
The breakers are white as foaming yeast,
  But sheltered safe and warm are we.

A gust of wind and a dash of rain,
  The storm has reached the coast at last,
The gale moans low like a thing in pain,
  Then shrieks and roars, a raging blast.

The waves sweep over the reeling deck,
  The vessel staggers in the sea,
She drifts in the trough a helpless wreck, —
  While warm and sheltered safe are we.

                        Newton Marshall Hall.

XII.

BESIDE THE SEA.

A Villanelle.

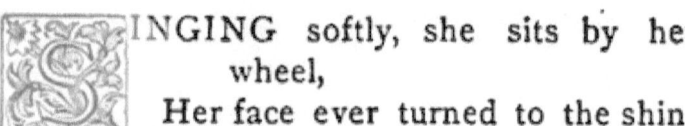INGING softly, she sits by her
        wheel,
        Her face ever turned to the shin-
            ing bay,
Long waiting the sound of his grating keel.

The table is spread for the evening meal ;
    Thro' the door streams the sleepy, golden
        day :
Singing softly, she sits by her wheel.

"My sailor's love is for woe and weal,
    Tho' my heart groweth sick at his delay,
Long waiting the sound of his grating keel."

"Our Lady of Grace," — chimes the Angelus'
        peal —
    "Star of the sea ! light my love on his
        way."
Singing softly, she sits by her wheel.

The bay gleams cold, like murderous steel,
  And still by the casement she keepeth her
     stay,
Long waiting the sound of his grating keel,

And ever, as if her heart to heal,
  Bows meekly her saintly head to pray;
Singing softly, she sits by her wheel,
  Long waiting the sound of his grating keel.

Daniel Luther Lawrence.

XIII.

WATCHING FOR THE FLEET.

ON Gloucester bluffs where the salt
        spray flies,
        And the surges beat,
        With anxious faces and straining
        eyes,
    For the missing fleet,
The fisher women their vigils keep.

They scan each sail on the gray sea's rim,
    And their cheeks grow white
As it fades away like a spectre dim
    In the waning light.
The wind blows chill and the breakers moan.

Oh, watch no more by the hungry deep;
    You will look in vain.
In ocean graves they are laid to sleep,
    And the hurricane
Above has chanted their requiem.

                        Newton Marshall Hall.

XIV.

AN ATOM.

N atom is a little thing,
  As small as small can be ;
'T is smaller than a needle's point,
'T is smaller than a flea.

I never saw one in my life ;
Yet, when I was in school,
I heard it would take two of them
To make a molecule.

Just think of something so minute
That on an inch of paper
Five thousand million could be placed,
Along with aqueous vapor !

The shape of them was never known,
Nor was the color either ;
In fact, that they are all a myth,
I am a firm believer.

XV.

EVENING.

O eastward, o'er the green, long shad-
    ows creep;
  The sunlight steals from vales in
    quiet sleep
To crown with mellow glow and tints, so deep,
    The distant height.

The night breeze, rising, hastens on apace;
It fans with cooling breath all Nature's face;
Low vespers float from quiet dells, through
    space,
      In upward flight.

Her trailing robes of light Day closer twines;
She sinks in glory o'er the distant pines,
And from her warm embrace the world con-
    signs
      To arms of Night.
             Walter Seager Sullivan.

XVI.

A WINTER'S DAY.

MORNING.

IS cold and chill; — the dull, gray
    sky
  Seems like an ice-arch o'er a deep
    ravine;
Straight up the smoke from that tall chim-
  ney curls —
Cold earth and colder heaven it lags between;
Beneath its icy fetters, all unseen,
  The buried streamlet, gently murm'ring,
    purls.

NOON.

  A wintry day! So thick the clouds
That Sol scarce shows us which are southern
    skies;
  But see! from yon far mountain-side comes
    down
A mighty host, that slow and silent flies
Across the frozen lake. Before our eyes
  The low-hung clouds take on a deeper
    frown.

EVENING.

Dark falls the night ; — in playful mood
The snow swift scurries o'er the dreary plain,
  Sports round the eaves ; while like a were-
    wolf's cry
The fierce wind loudly shrieks its weird re-
  frain ;
And yet, my love, I count the storm but gain,
  So bright the cosy hearth when thou art
    nigh.

Charles Frederic Robinson.

XVII.

ROSE MAY.

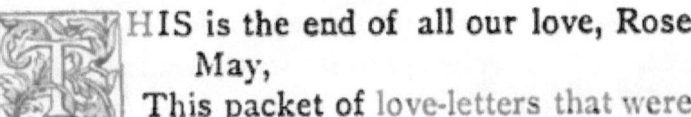HIS is the end of all our love, Rose
    May,
This packet of love-letters that were
    penned
Before I·thought that I should ever say
    "This is the end."

A year ago, and merely to defend
Your slipper from the wet some rainy day,
I would have dared the high gods to offend.

And now our summer dream has passed away,
For you are flirting with some other "friend,"
While I am singing in this idle lay
    "This is the end."

XVIII.

FAINT-HEART'S LAMENT.

HE would not take a kiss, — a miss
   Whose mouth was sweet with taunt-
     ing,
   Whose lashes swept o'er rose-lit
     cheeks
Where Cupid's flag was flaunting.

Ah, me ! the golden time went by.
   Her head, half turned, said plainly
That wishes such as mine that night
   Were running riot vainly.

But now — somehow — I 'm sure of this, —
   She would not take a kiss amiss.
              Wilder Dwight Quint.

XIX.

"SHE'S FAST ASLEEP."

SHE'S fast asleep, and silent I
    Behold her 'mongst the blossoms
       lie.
  She's careless grown, my lady fair,
  The gold-brown tresses of her hair
Down past her cheeks disordered fly.

Her parted lips the breath floats by, —
Her blossom lips which shape a sigh, —
  I would a smile were resting there!
    She's fast asleep.

I bend above her — who knows why?
Oh, would that I had power to try
  What many another man would dare!
  Down in the pillows, pink so rare,
Her cheek peeps up — shall I be shy?
    She's fast asleep!

William Byron Forbush.

XX.

HORTENSE.

Wherinne is showne ye craftinesse of her lover.

ORTENSE is haughtye, and no
smile
She **deignes to** shedde on me,
Although I love her to dispaire,
And serve her faythfullye.

Each mornynge, when ye **Sonne first shines,**
I from my couch doe springe ;
And to her Lattice windowe then
Dew sprinklede flouerets **bringe.**

And when she goeth to ye wode,
Downe through ye mossie dell ;
And with her lovelie armes doth drawe
Ye water from ye well,

I haste to followe after **her,**
Althoughe she tells **me nay.**
And when **I tell my love to her,**
She not a worde will say.

I toke her lytel hande in mine,
And quoth full softe and lowe ;
" Deare hearte, I must needes saye **farewell,**
I to ye **Warres** must goe."

Straightway her face **gat** deathlie **white,**
" O **Cyril** dear ! " quoth she,
" Nowe prithee doe not goe awaye,
Forsoothe, I — I love thee."

Frank John Urquhart.

XXI.

THE GARDEN.

DAHLIAS fill a wondrous garden;
    Peonies from the land of palms,
Radiant in their musky splendor ;
    Tulips with their gaudy charms.
Ah ! for me spring's daffodillies,
Not the summer's tiger lilies ;

For the gorgeous tiger lilies
    Are the dark-eyed belles of Spain,
And the peonies Eastern maidens
    With their passionate cheeks aflame.
What care I for tulips slender,
With their oriental splendor !

But within the gorgeous garden,
    In the angle of the wall,
Where the dewdrops still were clinging
    In a grassy tangle tall,
There I spied a rosebud hiding,
In its weedy bower confiding.

Modest bud, still **fresh** with morning,
  You are like a maid I know :
I will pass those gorgeous beauties ;
  They would stain a breast of snow.
I will pluck thee ; — go, sweet blossom,
She shall wear thee **on** her bosom.

                Fred *Lewis Pattee.*

XXII.

THE CHANGING YEAR.

RED as my sweetheart's lips
        Were the nodding heads of
        clover.
    Deep as my true-love's eyes
  The blue sky bending over.
All out of doors, both birds and men, were
        singing;
    The year was springing,
        And so was love.

The wintry sky is gray
  As the ash of a dying ember;
The snow falls white to-day,
  It is the chill November.
The breeze that sweeps the orchard floors is
        sighing,
    The year is dying,
        But not my love!

                    William Byron Forbush.

✳

XXIII.

THE FRESHMAN'S SOLILOQUY.

WONDER who that man can be
Now coming near! He seems to me
Like one who holds within his hand
The sun, the moon, the planets, and
Maintains this little world of ours
Obedient to **his sovereign** powers.
What stately mien and look **has he,**
Compared with men of **less degree!**
That must be "Prex," or some great Prof. —
I think I 'll take my hat quite off.

A Voice.

Oh, no, young sir,
You **greatly err!**
It **is the** college carpenter.

Ozora Stearns Davis.

XXIV.

TO A GLOVE.

 SIT here while the moments go,
Gazing up at a dingy glove;
And do I sentimental grow,
And murmur of some fickle love?
Well, no, not quite.

'T was white as foam on surging main,
But wear and tear made it succumb;
It now has many a crimson stain;
There also straggles from the thumb
Some old horse hair.

It helped me win the "light-weight" prize,
It and its mate which hangs close by;
Helped me to close up Thumper's eyes,
And get old Bangs "in chancery;"
That boxing glove.

XXV.

ON ROBERT HERRICK.

F hills and vales and dear melodious
    streams
    Within whose limpid depths cool
    shadows lie;
How meadow violets reflect the sky,
And how sweet mother earth with radiance
    gleams
And glows for happiness,—such are the
    themes,
O merry voice, in which thou dost outvie
The careless birds, that, soaring far on high
On wings of song, pour forth soft summer
    dreams
In liquid melody. Yet dost thou sing
Of love a higher strain. Not with chill art,
Like one who from afar examining
With calm philosophy, still stands apart
And smiles : its agonizing sorrows wring
Thy soul; its rapturous joys consume thy
    heart.

William Drummond **Baker.**

XXVI.

AS YESTERDAY, SO TO DAY.

 *FAIN would climb, but dare not,
        lest I fall.*"
        So wrote a gallant courtier of Queen
        Bess,
    In days of ruffs, peaked beards, and regal
        dress,
When Faery Queens were dainty maidens all,
    Each to her lover's guess.

He fain would climb!   For what ?   We may
        suppose
    His quick hand wandered to his jeweled
        blade,
    Eager for Spain's dark blood, in England's
        aid ;
Or else he dreamed to stand within the muses'
        close ;
    Or loved a maid.

But dare not!   Ah ! his courage failed him
        then :
    Yet blame him not o'ermuch: His hilt of
        gold

Might **ne'er** win cherished fame when all
 was told :
The wayward muses frowned **upon** his **up-**
 start pen ;
 The maid **was cold.**

And so we live a space, and fain would climb
 Like that **gay** cavalier in silken hose.
 We treasure up a smile or withered rose :
Then courage fails. What might be ours in
 heights sublime,
 Alas ! who knows ?

      Wilder Dwight Quint.

XXVII.

ON SEVERN'S PORTRAIT OF KEATS.

HAD I not known thy face, immortal
        one,
        And found unnamed this portraiture
        of thee,
    I might have hailed it as a fantasie ;
Or yet a thing that some wild brain had won
From misty region stranger to the sun ;
    I might have looked to see it fade or flee
    At mortal gaze, like folk of Arcady,
Or those sad shapes that flit when night is
        done.
The nameless pain in those deep eyes of thine,
    As in a dream far-gazing wistfully,
Sometimes I almost think that I could tell ;
And oft I fain would link that pain with mine,
    When all the world a pest-house seems to
        be,
And my dark fate flings over me her spell.

                                Fred Lewis Pattee.

XXVIII.

IN ROMAN DAYS.

" Cato literas Graecas aetate jam declinata didicit."
QUINTIL. 12, xi. 23.

 STRONG old man, whose soft and
silvered hair
Is tossing in the mild Italian air,
Walks **gravely** through **a marble**
colonnade ;
Upon his brow **his aged hand is laid,**
And now he stops, **and now he starts** again,
And whispers **in** despair, " εἶς, μία, ἕν."

Composed **and** stern the Romans were, they
say,
But **this old Porcian is disturbed** to-day.
The **wingèd hours in silent glee steal** by
And leave the baffled **sage with** κεν and και.
That modern days are **quite like those antique,**
We see from Marcus **Cato** learning **Greek.**
Ozora Stearns **Davis.**

XXIX.

VILLANELLE.

ναυσὶ δ' οὔτε πεζὸς ἰὼν κεν εὕροις
ἐς Ὑπερβορέων ἀγῶνα θαυματὰν ὁδόν.

Pyth. X.

ἔνθα
νᾶσος ὠκεανίδες
αὔραι περιπνέοισιν, ἄνθεμα δὲ χρυσοῦ φλέγει κ. τ. λ.

Olymp. II.

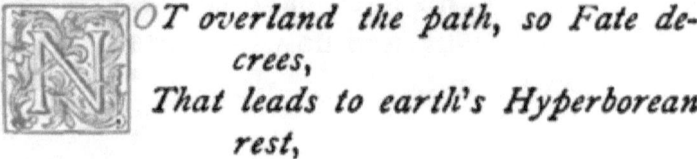OT overland the path, so Fate de-
    crees,
    That leads to earth's Hyperborean
    rest,
Nor over seas.

Thus sang the bard whose honeyed lips the
    bees
Had destined eloquent and lordliest;
Not overland the path, so Fate decrees.

The mystic fruit of the Hesperides
Men shall not find far down the golden west,
Nor over seas.

They dream a dream, a broad highway to ease,
A path to peace, to soothe their anguished
      breast;
Not overland the path, so Fate decrees.

But elsewhere seek the wisdom and the peace
Of pious souls.   Not here's the heavenly
      quest,
Nor over seas.

And to the isles where-round the ocean breeze
Blows breath of golden blooms, isles of the
      blest,
Not overland the path, so Fate decrees,
Nor over seas.

           Daniel Luther Lawrence.

XXX.

MOUNT MANSFIELD.

HOU grim old mountain ! did great
      Jove's stern might
    O'erthrow and bind thee here, at
      that dread time
When he struck down the Titans for their
    crime
Against his throne? I know not, but the
    sight
Of thy huge face, turned ever toward the light,
Suggests defiance. Thou art more sublime
Than all around thee here, where mountains
    climb
On top of mountains, rugged height on height;
Thy cheeks are scarred by lightnings, torn and
    seamed
By earthquakes ; gray and scanty is thy beard
Of stunted pines. Thy stern-set lips can vie
With Death in grimness. Often have I
    dreamed
Of thee as our Prometheus, bound and feared,
But stronger thou, to suffer and defy.

XXXI.

ON THE STATUE OF NIOBE.

ITH stone the gods once bound my
 heart,
And stopped each flowing vein;
Praxiteles with magic art,
Has made me live again.

XXXII.

MARLOWE.

HE cry of souls that perish in the
         night,
      The lightnings' blinding glare, the
         pine trees' dirge,
The solemn thunder of the breaking surge,
The march of armèd men, the bloody fight,
All these found voice in Marlowe's mighty
      line.
He could be gentle as a mother too.
What pity that the gifted singer threw
Such priceless pearls before the senseless
      swine
Of lust!   His life work only just begun,
To die the victim of a drunken brawl!
Who knows what precious thoughts he left
      untold,
What deathless fame his genius might have
      won,
Had he not blighted in his wretched fall
The fairest promise of the age of gold.

                    Newton Marshall **Hall.**

XXXIII.

TO MY TAMBOURINE.

TAMBOURINE, tambourine,
    Fairest gift of fairest queen,
    Hanging by thy silken band,
    Gorgeous from my lady's hand,
There is music in thy bells
That no tinkling ever tells.

Tambourine, tambourine,
Speak of her whom thou hast seen.
Art has many devotees;
Thou hast only one to please.
Flowers everywhere grow free,
But thy roses bloom for me.

Tambourine, tambourine,
Thou dost love her too, I ween.
Thou hast felt her gentle touch —
Who on earth, beside, has such?
Thou wilt sympathize with me,
Parted from her, here to be.

XXXIV.

TO LOVE, IMMORTAL LOVE.

O Love, immortal Love, my soul doth
    cry !
    Treading this lower plain of woes
      and cares,
  Vexed with entanglements of men's affairs,
  I search the encroaching mists with eager
    eye ;
And beaten down, yet long for wings to fly.
  I yearn with bitter tears and trustful
    prayers   .
  To reach that land where play the heavenly
    airs,
  And the fair vales of holy comfort lie.
Ah ! Love is perfect, and he does it wrong
  Who faultily and ignorantly sings,
  Calling on lips profane the holy fire ;
And so I pray the discords of my song
  May all be soothed by Him who tunes the
    strings
  To the sweet diapason of God's choir.
                William Byron Forbush.

XXXV.

VIOLINISTE.

UNDER your rounded chin
     The polished wood of your violin
     Comes lengthening down to your
          slender hand,
Where a bit of ribbon (a silken band)
Flutters and floats.   'T were better planned
     To be under your rounded chin.

     Now from your snowy throat
     Swells on the air a soft, sweet note ;
And, caught in a perfect chord by the strings,
Its cadence rises and falls and swings,
And I listen enrapt as the melody rings
     Up from your snowy throat.

     Deftly your fingers go
     O'er the quivering strings, now high, now
          low,
And words that speak from the music start,
And for me thrill the world in its every part,
     Until I feel that over my heart
     Deftly your fingers go.

Wilder Dwight Quint.

XXXVI.

RONDEL.

ITH bleeding feet and drooping head
　　Fair Love unto my wicket came;
　　And　faint　he　called　upon　my
　　　　name —
Ah ! how resist him as he plead ?

With wine of love sweet Love I fed,
　　With　honey　of　song, — and　who　would
　　　　blame ?
With bleeding feet and drooping head
　　Fair Love unto my wicket came.

Too well — ah me ! — I know the bread
　　I give him is my broken frame;
　　That my life feeds his altar-flame ; —
And yet, — and yet, when all is said,
With bleeding feet and drooping head
　　Fair Love unto my wicket came.
　　　　　　　　　　　Daniel Luther Lawrence.

XXXVII.

JUNE AND NOVEMBER.

Triolets.

H ! summer days steal by like happy
    dreams,
    And summer hours are minutes,
      love, with thee ;
When ripples softly murmur on the streams,
Oh ! summer days steal by like happy dreams.
Half faint with sweetness now the meadow
    seems,
    And joyous voices chant in every tree ;
Oh ! summer days steal by like happy dreams,
    And summer hours are minutes, love, with
      thee.

I 'm weary, love ! I would I were with thee ;
    I 'm all alone, while blow the night winds
      dreary ;
Lonely and sad the creeping hours flee ;
I 'm weary, love ! I would I were with thee.
The withered leaves flit o'er the barren lea ;

In sad November naught is gay and cheery.
I 'm weary, love ! I would I were with thee ;
  I 'm all alone, while blow the night winds
    dreary.

Fred Lewis Pattee.

XXXVIII.

THE SUMMER SCHOOL OF SCIENCE.

THERE lived a would-be physicist,
With bright blue eyes and curly hair;
To laws of dress and etiquette
He gave uninterrupted care.
At length to learn of Gramme's machine,
Of gravity and such as that,
Of waves of light, and microphones,
He forth did go to study at
　　　The Summer School of Science.

There lived a would-be chemistress,
Who firmly settled in her mind
That there were certain hidden things
Which she must really try to find;
Some molecules, some carbonates,
The true atomic weight of tin,
Precipitated atmosphere —
Of these she came to study in
　　　The Summer School of Science.

For physicist and chemistress
The summer season now is o'er.
Of their respective specialties
They know just what they knew before.
But how two bodies tend to meet,
And how two spirits coalesce,
And how two hearts can beat as one—
All this they learned, and so they bless
          The Summer School of Science.

XXXIX.

WEDDED.

BIRDS are singing in the closes, —
  Singing for joy of June.
  Scent of English violets
  Mingles with the mignonette's ;
And the garden 's red with roses,
  When the glad brown thrushes croon, —
Thrushes crooning in the closes
  All this rose-sweet June.

Rarer joy than yours has found me,
  Birds of the rose-sweet June !
Maidenhood with Maytime ended ;
Love, the strong one, o'er me bended,
And with orange blossoms crowned me
  In the hot, sweet summer noon.
Rarer joy than yours has found me, —
  Love's year has its June.

Richard Hovey.

XL.

IN SUNSET'S DEPTHS.

N sunset's depths, whose flushes
    come and go
  Across the silent **wastes** of driven
    snow,
Which tint blue heaven with splendors mani-
    fold,
And change grim mountain peaks to heaps of
    gold,
There lies the alchemy man cannot know,
Although each eve its working he behold
        In sunset's depths.

In sunset's depths, in which we almost see
Our fairy castles reared in childish glee,
There lies for me a stronger, better art, —
One able, in my weakness, to impart
Deep sense of strength and hope, inspiring,
        free.
Thus **lies the source of peace to my sad heart**
        In sunset's depths.

                    Ozora Stearns Davis.

XLI.

A THREAD OF GRAY.

S there a time from thoughts of sad-
   ness free ?
   An autumn cricket pipes his dirge
      in May,
And ere the springtime fades, on some lone
      tree
Are yellow leaves to whisper of decay.

This morn I found a single thread of gray
In golden locks once bright as autumn's
      moon.
Has springtime fled, and has the bright hey-
      day
Of morn and gladness faded into noon ?

Oh ! what were life, should love and joy be
      cold ?
But what is love when happy youth is dead ?
So I am gray, so I am growing old,
And happy youth forevermore is fled.

There is no time from thoughts of sadness
    free ;
We hail our joys and they at once are dead ;
The gentians bloom ere springtime violets
    flee,
And vespers come ere matin psalms are read.

                    Fred Lewis Pattee.

XLII.

SONGS WITHOUT WORDS.

WHEN one in silence long has brood-
    ing lain,
  A rush of melody on quivering wings
  Sweeps over him; and then he
    fiercely sings
His heart's own song of rapture or of pain.

But when the dream is past, and in the glare
Of open day with calmer brain he reads,
What seemed like nature's whispered secret
    needs
Interpreters; for naught but words is there.

Beyond dull words look thoughts; and thought-
    fulness
Has never seen those hills whose shining
    height
Magnificent is glowing in the light
Of paradise. This words cannot express.
                William Drummond Baker.

XLIII.

SPRING.

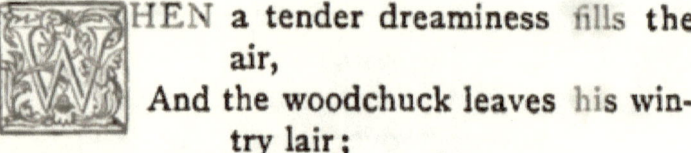HEN a tender dreaminess fills the
    air,
    And the woodchuck leaves his win-
       try lair;
When the slimy mud is everywhere,
And the base ball nine begins to swear,
Because the campus is not yet bare;
When the night resounds with the tin horn's
    blare,
And the student lays aside all care,
And every one feels like having a "tear,"
      Then it's spring.

XLIV.

THE MIST-WRAITH.

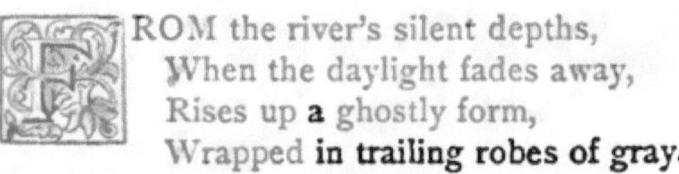ROM the river's silent depths,
When the daylight fades away,
Rises up a ghostly form,
Wrapped in trailing robes of gray.

'T is the Mist-wraith, pale and sad ;
O'er the landscape wide she creeps.
With her finger on her lips
At her silent task she keeps.

Fireflies light her on her way ;
Wood and field and village street
Thick she covers with her pall.
Passing on with noiseless feet,

Into chambers soft she glides,
As the midnight comes apace.
Restlessly the sleeper turns,
When she breathes upon his face.

Gone is she at break of day,
But her footsteps you may trace
By her garments left behind,
Soft and light as finest lace.

Newton **Marshall Hall.**

XLV.

SEA-SONG.

P and away! For the east wind is
     blowing,
     And high on the rocks dashes
     swift-driven spray;
Far in the distance the tempest is growing,
As we watch the approach of lowering day.

Up and away! At home they are waking
And hurrying down in the face of the gale,
While the glare from the east dims eyes that
     are aching
In search for a glimpse of an incoming sail.

Up and away! Though storm clouds are kiss-
     ing
The measureless waste of fierce-flying foam,
For the blasts that over our vessel are hissing
Are going before us to welcome us home.

                    William Drummond Baker.

XLVI.

DRIFT.

HAT came in with the tide to-day?
Bits of wood and seaweed gay,
Shells and moss and a broken oar,
Floating waifs from a foreign
    shore, —
Something else by the breakers rolled,
Something stark and white and cold,
Face upturned to the light of day.
Sullenly roars the sea with its prey.

                Newton Marshall Hall.

XLVII.

SONG.

HERE 'S a flush on the high western
    mountains,
And the forests in rapture awake ;
There 's a flashing of light in the
    fountains,
And a promise o'er valley and lake.

And the lover, who gloomily wanders
Through the morning's first beautiful flush,
In his hoping soul greedily ponders
O'er a promise, a song, and a blush.

Ozora Stearns Davis.

XLVIII.

AN AUGUST NOON.

THE swooning meadows lie like sum-
     mer seas ;
  The landscape reels ; a quivering,
     ghastly gleam
Bedims the fields ; — as in a spell they
     seem,
Save where the redtop rolls with scarce a
     breeze.
The mowers in the clover to their knees
  Seem threading out the mazes of a dream.
  No sound, save far away the locust's
     scream,
Or dreamily a bird-voice in the trees.

The cricket's monotone amid the grass
  Is scarcely heard, — a soothing lullaby, —
  And steady drones the summer-sounding
     bee.
The mingled notes to sleepy murmurs pass,
  Without a sound floats o'er a butterfly,
  And drowsiness and dreams steal o'er me.

Fred Lewis Pattee.

XLIX.

THE STORM.

THE wind has blown in icy gusts all
        day,
    And through this valley, once the
        dwelling-place
  Of sunny spring, now sweeps with **furious**
      pace.
The sun shines dim behind a **bank of gray,**
The trees and hills and **very heavens sway**
  With sickening rockings. **As I turn my**
      face,
    The eastern hills are gone. The wind-
        swept space
Below them only bending elms betray.
Hark! through the ceaseless roar the heavy
        boom,
  Half smothered, **of the** sunset **gun.** The
      form
Of objects long familiar **in** the gloom
  Is changed. Without, within, deep shad-
      ows swarm;
And as day sinks in blackness, in my room
  I listen shuddering to the whirling storm.

William Drummond Baker.

L.

BEHINDE YE ARRAS.

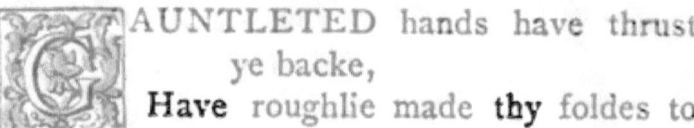

G AUNTLETED hands have thrust
  ye backe,
  Have roughlie made thy foldes to
  quake,
And thy quainte figures, golde and blacke,
Have caused to bow and swaye and shake,
Fantastic Arras.

A white-jowled knave with poniarde brighte,
With stealthie treade once soughte thee oute,
And lurked behinde thee in ye nighte,
Whilst ghostlie shadowes flocked aboute,
O grislie Arras!

Once, soe ye ancient legende goes,
In ye gode dayes of bluffe olde Hal,
A noble knighte hard-pressed bye foes,
Founde in thee safetie from them all,
O cunninge Arras!

This morn, when no one else was nighe,
Before ye men-at-armes awoke,

My Ladye, from her lattice highe,
Dropped downe a littel perfumed note,
O silente Arras !

And when ye birdes have gat to sleepe,
My Ladye Anne will meete me here,
When first ye moonbeames 'gin to peepe.
And now I waite her **cominge**, deare,
O lovelie Arras !

Frank John Urquhart.

LI.

THE BROKEN BANJO.

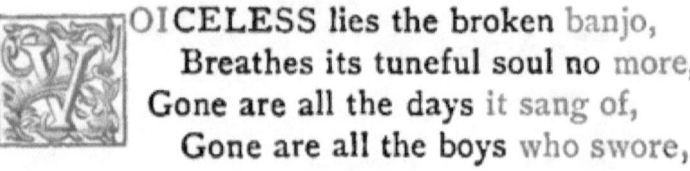OICELESS lies the broken banjo,
    Breathes its tuneful soul no more,
Gone are all the days it sang of,
    Gone are all the boys who swore,

When the banjo, loudly thrummed on,
    Roused them from their night's repose,
That the wretch who thus annoyed them
    Should be numbered 'mong their foes.

O thou past-recalling banjo!
    Would I might see, even now,
Other night-disturbing banjos
    Past recalling, e'en as thou.

               Warren Fenno Gregory.

LII.

HER PROMISE.

QUIT the dusty way,
  Where the elms uniting sway
    Just above;
  In deeper shadow there
Stands the form, **so dainty fair,**
  Of my **love.**

To me the laughing face,
With the most bewitching grace,
  Lightly trips.
I look, pause, reassure,
Ere I lift **a** face so pure
  To my lips.

She says, **with smile divine,**
On her birthday she **'ll be mine**
  Evermore.
She presses close to tell
Me her age, it is — ah, well !
  Only four.

Walter **Seager** *Sullivan.*

LIII.

AT THE CLUB.

Rondel.

WHEN a pretty maiden passes
    By the window down the street,
    Cards and billiards lose their
        sweet ;
Conversation on old brasses
Languishes ; up go the glasses : —
    " Nice complexion ! "   " Dainty feet ! "
When a pretty maiden passes
    By the window down the street.

Smith forgets the "toiling masses,"
    Robinson the fall in wheat ;
    All the club is indiscreet.
Ah ! the wisest men are asses
When a pretty maiden passes.

                            Richard Hovey.

LIV.

THE HERMIT THRUSH.

Rondel.

FAR, far away in evening's hush,
　　We caught a plaintive, liquid lay,—
The lonely love-lorn hermit thrush
　　That sang the vesper hymn of day.

The fragrant air was drunk with May,
While from the marsh's tangled brush,
Far, far away in evening's hush,
　　We caught a plaintive, liquid lay.

The mist stole from the meadows lush,
　　The day's glad chorus died away,
Save, half unheard, the river's rush,
　　And where, like murmurs from its spray,
Far, far away in evening's hush,
　　We caught a plaintive, liquid lay.

Fred *Lewis Pattee.*

LV.

ARBUTUS.

N mossy bank, in wet, pine-shaded
    nook,
  Where yet remain some patches of
    the snow
From which the rills with rippling music
  flow,
And swell each day some muddy, roaring
  brook,
Surging around its every bend and crook,
  Are found the buds that fairies hide below
  Dark, dying leaves, a careful covering, so
Each seeking eye the spot may overlook.
From something of the sunset in the fall,
  And some of winter's white when nature
    slept,   •
The elves had formed the flowers, and, at the
  call
  Of spring's returning robins, those who
    kept
The chaliced prison loosed the chains, and all
  This new-born beauty man can now accept.
                  Ozora Stearns Davis.

LVI.

THE LOTUS-EATERS.

HIS is a land of dreams. The hills
are gray
With haze, and silent streams glide
on with slow
And placid current. Ocean's ebb and flow
Sounds dead and passionless from far away.
The star-lit nights are voiceless, till the day
Shoots quickly from the sea. Dreamy and
low
Is nature's speech. Such is our world, and
so
We live in peace, nor work, nor love, nor pray.

When first we came, we loved this dreamy
land,
And love it now; yet sometimes, as to-day,
A breeze brings us across the rippling deep
A chill of keen remembrance. Up we stand,
While glazèd eyes grow fearful, and we say,
"O God! torture us not, but let us sleep."

William Drummond Baker.

LVII.

VITA NUOVA.

(Sonnetta doppa.)

ANTE ! when first I read the history,
    Enwrit herein by thee,
    Of all that infinite love that thou
        didst have
For Bice from the day when thou didst see ·
    First her sweet symmetry
And thy child heart was taken for her slave,
I was as one who sails across a sea,
    Elate of spirit and free
    As the glad gulls that laugh along the wave,
And hears the sirens singing fitfully
    A mystic melody,
Luring him to a melancholy grave.
With sweetest music, tender Florentine !
    Thou didst allure me through this little
        grove,
    And in the midst thereof
    Showed me a place where cypress-trees did
        twine
Their sombre ombrage ; yet I saw above
    An opening in the trees where-through did
        shine
    A ray of light divine,
Quivering with pulses of eternal love.

Richard Hovey.

LVIII.

THEOCRITUS.

A S those Swiss-dwellers in a northern
      clime,
    A-weary of the winter and its snow,
    Joyful, when cold and frost begin
      to go,
Hail the glad coming of the summer time;
Long, o'er their mountain **steeps,** again **to**
    climb
To hunt the eagle and the timid **doe,**
To pluck wild flowers that **in** deep valleys
    grow,
And drive their flocks home at the vesper's
    chime :
So oft, when tired of other Grecian song,
I hail thee gladly, and with thee alone
By some Sicilian stream I wander long
And hear the shepherds, in soft undertone,
Piping sweet ditties to a sylvan throng,
And feel the breath of southern breezes moan.
             Amos Cogswell Lyford.

LIX.

KRONOS.

S one of those huge monsters of the
        sky,
    Fierce with the flame of fiery float-
        ing hair,
Falls from the zenith through the upper air,
Hurling the planets from their paths on high,
Jarring creation from its harmony,
Spreading on earth destruction and despair,
Terrifying men to the temples and vain prayer;
So from the summit of his majesty
He falls, and heaven is shaken as flame;
        Zeus reigns
Usurping; and no matter what is left —
How smooth or tangled grows his god-life's
        weft —
With how swift footing or how slow the years
Speed on, for him forever there remains
A thunder and a chaos in the spheres.

                    Richard Hovey.

LX.

THE HEART.

*(**From the** German of Neumann.)*

WO chambers has the heart,
And Joy and Pain apart
    Dwell there.

In one Pain slumbers now:
Bid Joy awake with brow
    So fair.

O Joy ! speak light and low;
Let Pain no waking know:
    Have care.

Warren Fenno Gregory.

LXI.

"THE BRIDE OF DEATH."

S in a festering marsh, 'mid foul de-
        cay,
    A lily grows and sweetens all the
        air;
Or as some little primrose frail and fair
Springs from the blood shed on a battle day;
The house of Œdipus sent one sweet spray
    From out its slime and blackness and de-
        spair,
    Antigone, whose maiden soul could bear
The one fair bloom to drive its gloom away.

She dared to shed a sister's pitying tear,
    And leave her youth and love's bewitching
        breath
To do God's will; man's law she did not fear;
    She chose the right, — to be the "bride of
        Death."
Antigone, thy noble life still speaks,
The purest and the fairest of the Greeks.

                              Fred Lewis Pattee.

LXII.

"AD THALIARCHUM."

(*In Imitation of Horace.*)

HOW white Soracte yonder gleams
    'Mid snows 'neath which the trees
      are bending !
    The frost-king halts the rushing
      streams ;
Heap high the hearth, these chill bonds rend-
    ing.

Bring forth the wine : for gods, the tending
    Of winds that war the deep, one deems.
    How white Soracte yonder gleams
'Mid snows 'neath which the trees are bend-
    ing !

Let not the morrow haunt your dreams,
Nor spurn sweet loves : thee, boy, the spending
    Of eve in whispered tryst beseems,
The girl's glad laugh the love-pledge lending.
    How white Soracte yonder gleams
'Mid snows 'neath which the trees are bend-
    ing !

John Hiram Gerould.

LXIII.

IN MUD TIME.

HE summer has kissed the winter
    Across the face of spring;
    And Sol stood near and held the
        light,
And Tellus awoke and saw the sight,
And sprang from his mattress, bolt upright,
    And tore his coverlet all to strings,
    And quoted a number of hackneyed things,
Rebuking the maiden's wanton freak,
While rivers of tears flowed down his cheek,
And all he did in the following week
    Of any account, was to grumble and cry.
    But Luna, esteemed demure and shy,
    Leaned back her shoulders against the sky,
And snapped her fingers, and coughed, and
        said:
" I 'm laughing at Tellus, but really I 'm glad
That summer has once in kindness dared
    To kiss old winter in spite of his beard."

LXIV.

THREE SAILOR BOYS.

THREE fair-haired youths sailed out
to sea,
John and James and little Willyum ;
And they were sick as sick could be,
John and James and little Willyum.
Said James : " This is bad."
Said John : " This is sad."
But little Willyum, he said : " Gol dum."

These fair-haired youths were led to smile,
John and James and little Willyum ;
For they hoped that liquor might calm their
bile,
John and James and little Willyum.
Said John : " Currant wine."
Said James : " Cider 's mine."
But little Willyum, he said : " Drink rum."

These fair-haired youths got safe to shore,
John and James and little Willyum ;
And they swore an oath that they 'd sail no
more,

John and James and little Willyum.
John went to his bed,
James went to be fed,
But little Willyum, he went on a bum.

LXV.

LUNA.

(After Shelley.)

WHEN young stars sang and the blue
      vault rang
   In the centuries dim,
    To hail the birth of my sister Earth
  With celestial hymn,
I leaped with delight from my parent bright,
  I launched me far away,
And sped apace into airy space
  In maddening, joyous play.

I pined in tears a million years
  For flaming Mercury bold.
The strong, fierce fire of my great desire
  First languished, grew faint, then cold.
I, sorrowing, bowed my head so proud
  Upon my sister's breast,
And hid my woe in a mellow glow
  As our parent sank to rest.

A garland fair from the mists of air
  I weave as a festal crown,

As high in the skies I seem to rise
    On pillows of softest down.
I lead the stars in their airy cars
    With angel charioteers,
Through vast expanse in a mazy dance
    To the music of the spheres.

I peep o'er the brim of ocean's rim,
    With round and ruddy face ;
To my distant bath, a shining path
    With paving of gold I trace.
I mirror my beams in the silver streams,
    On ripple of lake and sea.
The sweetest notes from mortal throats
    Are poured out in rapture to me.

I pale on high in the cloudless sky
    When Aurora's car grows bright.
From heights serene, with silver sheen,
    I smile on the world at night.
I scorn in mirth all things of earth,
    From mortal greed I 'm free.
I hear but the beat of angels' feet,
    I shall live for eternity.

Walter Seager Sullivan.

LXVI.

"WITH FAIR FRENCH FORMS."

ITH fair French forms, in early days
By laughing poets lightly sung,
The sunny air with sweetness rung
Responsive to their mistress' praise.

And now the willing reader stays,
And sweetest strains he finds among
The books of ancient, curious lays
By laughing poets lightly sung.

The modern poets paraphrase
Old forms, awakened fresh and young,
And, not bewildered in the maze,
They play a harp as firmly strung
With fair French forms, in early days
By laughing poets lightly sung.

Ozora Stearns Davis.

LXVII.

DAY DAWN.

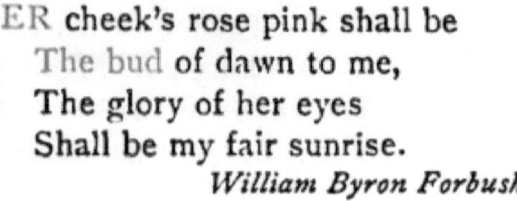ER cheek's rose pink shall be
The bud of dawn to me,
The glory of her eyes
Shall be my fair sunrise.

William Byron Forbush.

LXVIII.

A TREMBLING YES.

 TREMBLING yes ! How all my
pulses leap,
With joy and hope, awakened from
their sleep,
At that one word ! My life begins to-day,
For all those long, dark shadows clear away
Which fell across my path in darkness deep.

My own forever ! Ah ! swift blushes sweep
Across thy face, like rose-tints up the steep
Auroral sky. A kiss for lips which say
     A trembling yes !

The lagging days of waiting seem to creep
Like years, e'er I with thee can laugh and
    weep,
And weary oft, in memory's fields I stray,
To seek for flowers which bloom beside the
    way;
But finding many, only pluck and keep
     A trembling yes !

LXIX.

AT THE WINDOW.

O you were sitting and singing,
    As the evening chimes were ring-
        ing,
        At the window there;
And the quaint old-fashioned shading
Of the window curtains fading
        Made a picture rare.

Long I stood and looked and listened
While the dying sunbeams glistened
        In your golden hair;
Till the shades of night up-creeping
Took you into their own keeping
        I stood watching there.

Often since in vain I 've waited
Thinking that you were belated,
        Watching for my fair;
But the quaint old-fashioned shading
Of the window curtains fading
        Only mocked me there.

                    Henry Richard Foster.

LXX.

MY LADY IN THE GARDEN.

UT through the blossoms she's wan-
   dering slowly,
  Down in her pathway the apple-
   blooms fall,
With scent of the lilacs the air is made holy
 For her who is blossom and queen of them
  all.

Cover your heads and hide in the grasses,
 Lilies that nod so stately and tall.
She gathers you up in her hands as she
  passes, —
 They are whiter than you; she is queen of
  you all.

Kneel ye, pink roses; she's found out the
  treasure
 Of all your sweet incense down here by the
  wall;
Close to her cheek, if that be her pleasure, —
 It is pinker than you; she is queen of you
  all.

We, like the birds in the maple-trees o'er her,
  Follow her footsteps, we come at her call.
Only with that which is pure we 'll adore
      her, —
  She, the white blossom, the queen of us all.

                            William Byron Forbush.

LXXI.

TO POLLIE CONN^E.

ESHREWE me, thoughe I 'me
   forced to Woo
Miss Poll, I love Her notte;
   For all She talkes of ys Wage due,
Rente, Profit & all thatte.

I write to Her? Credit me, Noe!
Toe saye Soe were a Fibbe,
The onlie Wrytinge yt I doe
Is inne ye lytel Cribbe.

Frank John Urquhart.

LXXII.

HE IS OUR PEACE.

 HEAVENLY Father, fold me close
to Thee.
I look up in Thy peaceful eyes to-
night
With naught in mine but an unreasoning
fright,
And nestle like a bird that would be free.
Then, tired even of this, all wearily
I shade my face from the too-dazzling light
Upon Thy breast, and long if I but might
Forever in this haven cradled be.
Oh, what is there in the hot streets of life
Whereon I wander that can give me peace,
Or where can I lie down, assured of rest?
Without I hear but noise and din of strife,
The howl and wail and cries that never
cease;
Within, the stillness of Thy holy breast.

William Byron Forbush.

LXXIII.

"TENDER AND TRUE."

A Rondeau.

ENDER and true." **So** read that Douglas' **shield**
Who bore **the** heart of Bruce from the alien field
Back to his realm, **the land of cold and** dearth, —
Fairest to **him** within **the** wide **world's** girth,
Whose woes **it** was his glory **to** have healed.
Prouder this act of Douglas than **to** wield
A realm, nobler upon his arms annealed
This fair **device** than all the boasts of earth,
" Tender **and** true."

God grant that on my **heart** it may be sealed,
And in His grace grant my life, too, **may yield**
This surest stamp and print of gentle birth,
This crown and **flower** of all knightly worth,
This sum of Christian virtue here revealed —
" Tender and true."

Daniel Luther Lawrence.

LXXIV.

A BALLADE OF GRAVES.

 TANGLED wild rose climbs each
        mound,
        And white and red the clovers
        pave
The grass-grown avenues.   No sound
    In this enchanted city, save
    The murmuring of winds that wave
The unshorn locks of grass, the hum
    Of honey-bees holding conclave,
At last the roll of the evening drum.

A march on which all men are bound
    Is life, and all alike must brave
Its heat and burden, whether crowned
    With diadem or fool's cap, slave
    Or king.   Let only cowards crave
Some painless sweet viaticum
    Against the toil He willed, who gave
At last the roll of the evening drum.

Sweet is their slumber, and profound,
    Who here have laid aside the glave,

And pitched their lowly tents, where round
  Them only now the wild winds rave,
  And only rains from heaven lave
Their restful couch. This is the sum
  Of joy to hear, when near the grave,
At last the roll of the evening drum.

Envoy.

Ye peaceful dead, with this engrave
  Our hearts, too oft to such truth numb, —
For all men comes, or noble or knave,
At last the roll of the evening drum.

Daniel Luther Lawrence.

LXXV.

HARMONY.

 SET my trembling heart at tune
with Thine
To play upon its silent, throbbing
strings :
The sweetest anthems that my spirit sings
Are those the fullest of the breath divine.
Let but my feebler harp below combine
With Thine, which hymns the purest, ho-
liest things,
My soul with strains of heavenly music
rings,
Because Thy song is feebly sung in mine.
And though, while chanting at my very best,
Compared with those serene immortal notes
My weaker tone harsh and discordant be,
And only crudely, humanly expressed, —
Like the lark's song, I know it upward floats
To heaven, because inspired alone by Thee.

William Byron Forbush.

When even comes, a deep and holy calm
Falls softly over forest, hill, and stream;
The weary earth sends up its softened psalm
Of praise for rest, and like a varied dream
The dying day's quick joy and tumult seem.
When deeper shadows mark the closing day,
And ere the final ring of curfew, may
These songs bring back a sense of morning's
     light,
Of friends and scenes forever passed away,
And soften shades that swiftly close in night.